Magic Kitten

Picture Perfect

To Mowgli—the gray-and-white scrabbler.

GROSSET & DUNLAP
Published by the Penguin Group
Penguin Group (USA) LLC, 375 Hudson Street, New York, New York 10014, USA

USA | Canada | UK | Ireland | Australia | New Zealand | India | South Africa | China

penguin.com
A Penguin Random House Company

Text copyright © 2008, 2014 Sue Bentley. Illustrations copyright © 2008 Angela Swan. Cover illustration copyright © 2008 Andrew Farley. All rights reserved. First printed in Great Britain in 2008 by Penguin Books Ltd. First published in the United States in 2014 by Grosset & Dunlap, a division of Penguin Young Readers Group, 345 Hudson Street, New York, New York 10014. GROSSET & DUNLAP is a trademark of Penguin Group (USA) LLC. Printed in the USA.

Library of Congress Cataloging-in-Publication Data is available.

ISBN 978-0-448-46796-2   10 9 8 7 6 5 4 3

Picture Perfect

SUE BENTLEY

Illustrated by Angela Swan

Grosset & Dunlap
An Imprint of Penguin Group (USA) LLC

★ Prologue ★

The young white lion brushed against the tall grass as he padded down into the valley. Flame lifted his head, enjoying the smells of red soil and hot, dusty air. It felt good to be home.

Suddenly a terrifying roar rang out. "Ebony!"

As a powerful dark shape rose up from the shadow of some thorn trees, Flame froze. He should have known it wasn't safe to come back. He needed to find somewhere to hide from his uncle.

A bright flash lit up the valley, and a shower of silver sparkles fell where the young white lion had stood. In its place now crouched a tiny, fluffy chocolate-brown kitten. Flame's kitten heart beat fast as he lowered himself onto his belly and crawled behind a fallen tree.

A huge paw, almost as big as Flame was now, reached out of nowhere and scooped up the kitten.

Flame bit back a whine of terror as he was dragged deeper into the tangle of branches. Uncle Ebony had found him! He was finished.

But a kindly face with a scarred muzzle looked down at him. "Prince

Chapter
ONE

Orla Newton's dad flapped the newspaper in the air like a fan, so that it ruffled Orla's short hair.

"Da-ad! Don't! This movie's just getting to the good part! The aliens are about to take over the earth!" Orla complained, glued to the TV screen.

"Judging by all the sci-fi films

you watch, they've already taken over your body!" Mr. Newton joked, plonking the paper in her lap.

"Ha-ha, very funny!" Orla said, making a face as she reluctantly pressed PAUSE on the DVD remote.

She looked down at the article her dad had circled with a black felt-tip pen. "'Wildlife-photography competition for local children up to ten years old. Grand prize of a top-of-the-line digital camera and lots of prizes for runners up,'" Orla read aloud.

At the mention of a brand-new camera, she felt a flicker of interest.

Mr. Newton grinned at the look on his daughter's face. "Aha! I thought that would get your attention. Are you interested in it, then?"

Orla shrugged. "There's no point. My old camera's useless."

"No problem. I'll lend you mine," her dad said. "And I can give you a few tips on taking good pictures."

"Really?" Orla felt herself starting to warm to the idea.

"You're going on a school trip to Borton Pits Nature Reserve on Friday, aren't you? Sounds like the perfect place to get some photos," Mr. Newton said enthusiastically.

"I suppose I could—"

"Guess what? I've been picked for the county cross-country team!" an excited voice interrupted.

Orla turned around to see her sister, Grace, come bouncing into the living room, her blond ponytail flying out behind her.

At twelve, Grace was two years older than Orla. She practically lived at the after-school recreation center. Orla had been to it once, but they only seemed interested in kids who were really good at sports, so she

hadn't bothered going again.

"That's wonderful news! Well done,
sweetheart." Mr. Newton came over to
give Grace a hug.

"Yeah. It's great," Orla said quietly.

Grace pirouetted across the room
to the cabinet that held the silver
trophies she'd already won for tennis and
swimming. Straightening her shoulders,

she bent her neck and smiled proudly as if an invisible judge was looping a medal on a ribbon over her head.

Orla bit back a grin. Grace was such a drama queen! She couldn't help feeling a tiny stir of jealousy, though. It didn't seem fair that her sister was great at every sport she took part in, while Orla wasn't any good.

"Dad? Did you mean it about lending me your camera?" Orla asked on impulse.

"You bet. I'll go and get it right now," Mr. Newton said, smiling as he went into the hall.

"Why do you need to borrow Dad's camera?" Grace asked, frowning.

Orla explained about the wildlife-photography competition.

"Huh! You'd better take care of Dad's camera better than you did his fancy sunglasses," Grace said with a chuckle.

Orla felt herself blushing. "I didn't mean to sit on them. It was an accident."

"Yeah, like when you dropped that cake Mom had just made for Gran's birthday!" Grace reminded her gleefully.

"That wasn't my fault. I tripped over your sports bag that *you* left lying around!" Orla shot back.

"Are you two arguing again?" their mom asked, popping her head around the door.

"No, Mom!" Orla and Grace chorused.

"Hmm." Mrs. Newton didn't look convinced. "I'm about to make supper.

Anyone want to give me a hand?"

"Sorry, I can't. Dad's going to show me how to use his camera," Orla said quickly. "But Grace will help, won't you?"

"I don't mind," Grace said sweetly, but as their mom withdrew her head, she turned and stuck out her tongue at Orla. "I don't know why you're bothering with this competition! You never stick with anything—except for watching those pathetic movies about bug-eyed aliens!"

"So? They're really good. And I *will* stick with this. Just watch me!" Orla shot back at her. How hard could it be to point a camera at some silly old birds and butterflies, after all?

On Friday morning, Orla stood in a muddy clearing in Borton Pits while Miss Bussell divided the class into groups. Two classroom monitors, wearing green jackets, stood nearby.

"I hope we're not going to be in Bossy Bussell's group," Joe Manners commented. Joe lived two streets away from Orla and was her best friend in class.

Orla grinned. Miss Bussell was really nice, but she didn't put up with any nonsense—especially from Joe.

One of the monitors came over to Orla's group. "Hi! I'm Emma. I'll be showing you around," she said, smiling.

"Great!" Joe said, looking relieved.

"I hope you've all remembered to bring your cameras," Emma said, as the group moved off. "You'll want to

get a head start on taking photos,
with your whole school taking part
in this local photography competition.
I expect there'll be lots of fantastic
entries."

As Orla fished around in her school
bag for her camera, she noticed Joe
stuffing his hands into his pockets.
"Where's your camera? Didn't you
bring it?" she asked him.

Joe shrugged. "Yeah, but I can't
be bothered with this stupid contest.
We've got no chance of winning
with ten million other kids going in
for it."

"Don't be a wimp! My dad always
says you have to be in it to win it!"
Orla teased.

"Who are you calling a wimp?"

Joe said indignantly, but he took out his camera.

Orla and Joe followed the others along treelined paths. Birdsong filled the air and blue and yellow wild flowers dotted the grass on either side. As they reached the lake, Emma paused and began pointing out interesting ducks and geese.

Orla switched the camera on, trying to remember which setting to turn the dial to. *Dad said to use "automatic focus,"* she thought, *but which one's that?*

Suddenly there was a loud splashing noise. Two swans seemed to come running across the lake's surface on their black webbed feet, their powerful wings flapping as they prepared for takeoff.

"Wow! Look at that!" Joe said, aiming his camera.

All around Orla there were flashes and faint clicks as the other kids took photos of the swans. Orla twiddled the dial in a panic. Just as the swans took off, she raised her camera and pressed the button.

Nothing happened. She'd forgotten to take off the lens cap!

"Wasn't that fantastic? I think I got some great shots!" Joe said excitedly.

"I didn't! I missed the whole thing," Orla said, exasperated. "That's typical of me. I think I need some serious practice with this camera! I'm going over here by myself for a little while."

"Okay. See you later," Joe said.

Orla pushed through some trees and went down a bank. She found a quiet sunny spot ringed with tall reeds, away from the others. Not far away through the trees, she could hear Emma saying, "That duck with a wide bill is a shoveler, and those others . . ."

Orla spotted a robin on a branch. She quickly aimed the camera and pressed the button, but just captured

a blurry shot of the bush as the robin
flew away. She had no better luck with
a mallard, which decided to dive under
just as she took its photograph.

"This really isn't going very well!"
she grumbled.

A handsome black-and-white
duck came out of the reeds and began
paddling about. *Third time's a charm*,
Orla thought, moving closer.

Holding her breath, she crept
slowly down the grassy slope toward
the duck, but she wasn't looking where
she was going and her foot snagged on
a bramble, catching Orla completely by
surprise.

"Oh!" Orla stumbled and the
camera slipped from her fingers. It fell
to the ground and bounced down the

slope. She watched it in horror as it fell into the lake with a faint plopping sound.

"Dad will go crazy!" she groaned. Her heart sank even more as she imagined Grace's gloating face when she heard about the camera disaster.

Suddenly there was a bright flash and a shower of silver sparks shot over Orla's head into the lake. To her amazement, the camera slowly rose up out of the water, floated back through the air, and landed in her waiting hands!

Chapter
TWO

Orla clutched the camera in numb fingers, trying to make sense of what had just happened.

"I hope that I was in time to stop your little silver box from being damaged," mewed a tiny voice.

Orla whipped around in surprise. "Who's there? Who said that?"

"I did," answered the same voice.

Orla looked up the grassy slope
and saw a tiny, fluffy chocolate-brown
kitten with bright emerald eyes sitting
on a nearby log. Its fur glittered in
the sunlight, as if it was dotted with
hundreds of tiny diamonds.

Orla gazed at the kitten in complete
amazement. "D-did you just answer me?"

The kitten nodded. "My name is

Prince Flame. What is yours?"

"I-I'm Orla Newton," Orla
stammered.

The kitten pricked its tiny brown
ears. "I am pleased to meet you, Orla. I
have come from far away."

"Wow! Are you from another
galaxy?" Orla asked, excitedly thinking
of all her sci-fi films. "I bet a horrible
alien from the planet Zarg or somewhere
is after you!"

"I do not know of these aliens."
Flame's brown whiskers began to tremble
with fear. "But I am in danger. My uncle
Ebony has sent spies to find me. He
wants to keep the Lion Throne he stole
from me."

Orla blinked at Flame. Now that
the weird sparkles in his coat seemed

to have died down, Flame certainly
looked like an earth cat. In fact, with
his fluffy, rich brown fur, huge green
eyes, and alert pricked ears, Flame
was the most gorgeous kitten she had
ever seen.

She felt a surge of protectiveness
toward him. "Lion Throne? Don't
you mean Kitten Throne?" she asked
gently.

"I will show you!" Flame lifted his
tiny head proudly, and there was another
bright silver flash and a spray of sparks
as he jumped off the log.

"Oh!" Orla blinked, blinded for
a moment. When she could see again,
she saw that the tiny brown kitten
had vanished, but in its place stood a
magnificent young white lion. Tiny

points of light glittered in its thick velvety fur like a million rainbows.

"Flame?" Orla gasped, eyeing the lion's huge teeth and sharp claws. She stepped back hastily.

"Yes, Orla. It is me. Do not be afraid," Flame answered in a deep, gentle growl.

Before Orla could get used to the regal young lion, there was a final silver flash and the fluffy chocolate-brown kitten stood there in its place once more.

"Wow! You really are a lion prince. That's so cool!" Orla exclaimed.

Flame blinked up at her again and she saw that his tiny kitten body was beginning to tremble with fear again. "I must find somewhere to hide.

Will you help me, Orla?"

Orla's heart went out to Flame.
As a young white lion he was scary
and impressive, but as a kitten he was
adorable. "Of course I will! I'll take
you home with me," she said, bending
down and picking him up.

Flame began purring softly as she stroked his fluffy little head.

There was a rustling sound behind Orla. Flame tensed against her as someone pushed through the trees.

"I bet it's only Joe. He's my friend. He's going to be *so* surprised when I tell him about you!" Orla said excitedly.

"No! No one must know my secret," Flame told her, his face serious. "You must promise me."

Orla felt disappointed that she couldn't share her marvelous discovery with Joe, but if it helped keep Flame safe she was willing to agree. "All right. Cross my heart."

Seconds later, Joe appeared. "Did you manage to get your camera to work?" he said, and then his eyes

widened as he saw Flame. "Where did
you get that kitten from?"

"I just found him. He told me
he's called Fla—" Orla stopped hastily,
realizing that she was going to have to
be a lot more careful about keeping
Flame's secret. "I mean I've decided to
call him Flame," she went on. "We're
miles away from any houses here, so he
must be a stray. I'm taking him home
to live with me."

Joe reached out to stroke Flame's
ears. "Aw, he's really cute. I like his
name. If your parents won't let you
keep Flame, I'll take him."

"Sorry, no chance!" Orla held Flame
close.

Joe grinned. "Fair enough. Finders
keepers." He frowned suddenly. "You'll

never get Flame past Bossy Bussell. She
has eyes in the back of her head."

Orla thought hard. "I'll hide him
in my school bag. He's going to have
to stay very still and quiet until school
ends, aren't you?" she said gently,
looking meaningfully at Flame as she
opened her bag.

Flame gave a tiny nod. He jumped straight inside her bag and curled up next to her schoolbooks.

"That's one smart kitten," Joe said admiringly. "It's like he knew what you just said."

Orla bit back a grin. If only Joe knew!

"Bye. Have a good weekend!" Orla called to Joe after school, as she left him at the end of her road.

"We're going off to visit my grandma as soon as I get home, so I'll call for you before school on Monday," he called back. "Take good care of Flame!"

"I will!"

Orla held her school bag in her arms so she wouldn't jostle Flame as she walked up to her house and went inside. "Hi! I'm home," she called.

"Hi." Grace was sitting at the kitchen table with a glass of milk and some cookies. She was reading a sports magazine and didn't look up as Orla came in.

"Where's Mom?" Orla asked.

"On her way back from the store by now," Grace said, munching.

"Grace, I've got something to show you." Orla lifted Flame out of her bag and cradled him in her arms. "This is Flame."

"What?" Grace glanced up with a bored expression, but her face changed as soon as she saw Flame. "He's so cute! Whose is he?" she crooned, rubbing Flame under his chin.

"Mine," Orla said proudly. "He's a
stray. I found him, and he's going to live
here with me."

Grace's smile faded. "No way!
Remember when I wanted a puppy last
year? Mom and Dad said it wasn't fair
to have one because we're all out all day.
That goes for kittens, too!"

Orla felt her heart sink as she
realized that Grace was right. She
carefully put Flame back into her bag,
before shouldering it again and going
into the hall. "I'm just going back out
for a minute. I won't be long," she
called.

"Where are you going?" Grace
called back suspiciously, but Orla already
was closing the front door.

Orla wracked her brain as she

walked back down the street. There
was no way she was going to abandon
Flame. "I can't take you over to Joe's,
even if I wanted to. He'll have gone to
his grandma's by now. And now that
Grace knows about you, I can't hide
you in my bedroom," she told Flame
miserably.

Flame blinked at her from inside
her bag. "But I can hide myself. I will
use my magic so that no one except
you will be able to see and hear me."

"Really? You can make yourself
invisible?" Orla stopped in her tracks.
"That's fantastic. So you *can* live with
me and no one ever needs know—not
even Grace. Yay!"

She hurried back toward her house.
As she came in, she found her mom

in the kitchen unpacking the groceries.
Grace was helping to put stuff away.

"I've just been telling Mom about
your kitten," Grace said right away.

"What kitten?" Orla said innocently.

Grace scowled at her. "Duh! That
one you just brought in and told me
you were keeping!"

"Now, Orla? You know how we feel about having pets . . . ," her mom said firmly.

"I know. It was, um . . . a joke about me keeping him . . ." Orla faltered, and then she had a sudden flash of inspiration. "Flame really belongs to Joe Manners. I've just taken him back over there. I was only playing a trick on Grace!" she said, heading straight for the stairs before anyone asked any awkward questions. "I'm going up to do my homework now!"

Grace followed her to the bottom of the stairs. "You made me look silly. Why would you do that?"

"Serves you right for tattling!" Orla said, giggling.

In her bedroom, she made a cozy nest for Flame on her comforter. "There, you're safe now. Even if Grace calls Joe's house to check up on me, she won't get any answer! I'm so glad you're going to live with me," she told him.

"I am glad, too." Flame gave an extra loud purr and began pedaling the comforter with his tiny brown front paws.

Chapter
THREE

"How was the trip to Borton Pits?"
Mr. Newton asked later as Orla came
back downstairs after smuggling a piece
of fish from supper up to Flame.

"It was okay," she replied. "A nice
classroom monitor called Emma
showed us around. We saw lots of ducks
and stuff."

"Let's have a look at your photos, then.

Did you manage to remember what I told you about zooming in and getting things in focus?"

"Not exactly. I got a little confused," Orla admitted. She went to grab the camera. "The photos aren't very good. I need a lot more practice . . . ," she began reluctantly as she walked back into the living room with the camera.

Grace lunged forward and snatched it out of her hands. "Let's have a look!" she said, skipping across the room and plopping herself down next to her dad.

Orla wandered over slowly. She stood behind the sofa, watching over their shoulders as her dad scrolled through her photos.

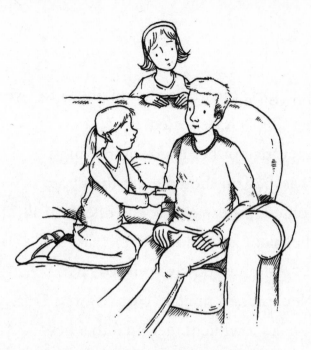

"Oh look, it's a super-boring old
bush!" Grace shrieked, pointing to the
screen. "And a bit of lake! I think I might
faint with excitement!"

Orla bit her lip, feeling her face
grow hot. There were only two photos,
and they were both terrible. But she
could hardly explain that after finding
Flame, she'd been too excited to take
any better ones.

"Orla can't take a good photo to save her life!" Grace teased.

Orla put her hands on her hips. "Maybe you should enter the photo contest, instead. You're the one with all the talent around here!"

"Simmer down, you two," Mr. Newton said mildly. "Don't worry, Orla. It takes a while to get used to a new camera." He got up and went toward the door. "I've got you something that might give you some ideas. I dropped by Andy and Bex's house on the way home from work."

Uncle Andy and Auntie Bex were Orla's favorite relatives. They were big fans of wildlife and had a huge garden with a wildflower meadow, a pond, and dozens of bird feeders.

Her dad returned with a pile of wildlife magazines. "There you go," he said, handing them to her.

Orla gave him a hug. "Thanks, Dad! These are great. I'll go up to my room and have a look at them right now!"

"As if *that's* going to make any difference," Grace murmured.

Mrs. Newton came in, jangling her car keys. "Ready to go to the rec center, Grace?"

"Coming!" Grace picked up her cute gym bag and swept out of the room. "Later, everyone!" she called over her shoulder.

Orla didn't answer her. She ran upstairs to find Flame sitting on her rug, licking his lips after finishing his supper. Orla threw herself down beside him and began leafing through the magazines.

"Some of these photos are awesome. Look at this one, Flame," she said, showing him a picture of a wood mouse.

Flame pricked his ears. His tail twitched excitedly and he jumped onto the page, patting at the mouse

with a tiny front paw.

Orla giggled. "It looks almost real, doesn't it? Look at this sunset and this close-up of a red poppy! I didn't realize that ordinary things could look so special." She sat up as an idea came into her head. "Come on! We're going out."

As Orla jumped to her feet, Flame tilted his head. "Where are we going?"

"To ask Dad if I can go to the park. I'm going to make a real effort at taking photos!"

As Orla walked the short distance to the nearby park, Flame trotted along at her heels, invisible to everyone except her.

It was a warm evening. There were people walking dogs in the park and some boys playing football. Four girls who looked about twelve years old were hanging out around the children's playground.

Orla was ready with her camera this time. She looked around for something to photograph and immediately spotted a squirrel near some trees.

Flame had seen it, too. He froze in a

crouch and his bottom wriggled excitedly
as he got ready to spring at it.

"No! Don't chase it, Flame! I want to
take its photo," Orla whispered urgently.

Flame gave a soft mew of
disappointment, but lay down obediently.
Orla aimed the camera at the squirrel
and started to press the button slowly.
But the squirrel was wary of Flame. It
bounded across the grass and shot
straight up a tree.

"I don't think I got it. Never mind.
I'll try a few unusual close-ups, like in
those magazines," Orla decided. She
took a few photos of daises and clover,
but somehow she couldn't seem to get
inspired by flowers.

As she straightened up, she noticed
that the four older girls from the kids'

playground were coming toward her.
The tallest of them, a blond girl, was
only a few feet away now. "Give us a
turn with your camera!" she called.

"Sorry, I can't. It's my dad's," Orla
said.

"So what? He isn't going to know,
is he?" said another girl.

"Yeah! So give us a turn with it,
or we'll help ourselves!" called the
blond girl.

Orla's tummy lurched. The girls
all looked tough, and they were a lot
bigger than she was. She wasn't going
to stay and argue with them.

"I've got to go now!" she called
out, stuffing the camera into her
shoulder bag. "Come on!" she said
urgently to Flame.

"Hey! Come back!" Orla heard pounding feet behind her as the older girls chased after her.

Orla and Flame raced across the park.

Flame started to fall back behind Orla. He was running fast, but his tiny legs couldn't keep up. Orla stopped and went back for him. Picking him up, she started running again, but she'd lost time and she couldn't run as fast with Flame clutched to her chest.

The older girls were gaining on her.

There was a thick clump of oak trees some distance away at the back of the park. Orla broke into a sprint and quickly veered toward them. Gasping for breath, she reached the

trees and rushed behind one of their
thick trunks.

Seconds later, she heard leaves
crunching as the four girls crashed in
after her.

Suddenly Orla felt a warm prickling
feeling down her spine. Her palms

fizzed gently as bright sparks ignited
in Flame's chocolate-brown fur and
his whiskers crackled with electricity.
Something strange was about to happen!

Chapter
FOUR

Time seemed to stand still.

Silver sparks swirled around Orla and Flame, spinning faster and faster, until it seemed as if they stood inside a glittering Christmas snow globe.

Orla's whole body tingled and her arms and legs felt all light and wobbly. A blur of brown trunk and leafy branches whooshed past her.

Orla blinked. She seemed to be
sitting on a branch, high at the top of
one of the oak trees. All around were
thick branches with big oak leaves.

Orla gulped hard and clung on
tightly.

"I won't let you fall," Flame mewed,
crouched on a smaller branch next
to her.

Down on the ground, Orla could
see the tops of the girls' heads as they
checked behind each tree for her.

"Where did she go?" Orla heard
the blond girl ask in frustration. The
others stood scratching their heads and
looking puzzled.

Orla forgot her fear of being so
high up and stifled a giggle. *This is
amazing*, she thought.

Looking out, she could see the
whole park—people walking their
dogs, the football game still going on,
and children playing on the swings.

Another cloud of sparks whizzed
around her and there was a rushing
sensation. Orla found herself on the

grass at the opposite side of the
park. She looked down at the fluffy
chocolate-brown kitten, rubbing
himself against her ankles.

"Wow! That was amazing, Flame!
I *loved* being up that high!" she said,
picking him up and cuddling him.
"Those mean girls were totally
confused. Thanks so much."

"You are welcome. I am glad
I was able to help," Flame purred
happily. "Thank you for coming back
for me, when I could not keep up
with you."

"I'd never let anyone hurt you,
Flame!" Orla told him. "But we'd
better go straight home. I don't want
to bump into them again. I can walk
more quickly if you get into my bag."

Flame nodded. He jumped inside
and then poked his head out of the open
zipper to look around as Orla set off and
hurried home.

"Any luck taking pics in the park,
sweetie?" Mrs. Newton asked as Orla
came into the living room.

She was back from dropping Grace
at the rec center and was watching her
favorite game show on TV. Mr. Newton
was reading a newspaper. He looked
over and raised his eyebrows in a silent
question.

"Not really, but it was good practice,"
Orla told them casually.

She hid a smile, imagining her
parents' look of shocked amazement
if she told them about balancing at the

very top of one of the enormous old oak trees. "I think I'll make some hot chocolate and go up to my bedroom. I'm going to read a bit before bed. Anyone else want a hot drink?"

"No thanks, dear. We've just had one," her mom said. "I'll come up and say good night to you later."

In the kitchen, Orla made the hot chocolate. She poured some milk for Flame and took it upstairs with her. He lapped it up with his little pink tongue, purring with enjoyment, before jumping onto her bed and curling up next to her.

Orla stroked his soft fur as she looked through some more magazines. "I love having you living here with me," she told him.

Flame looked up at her. His eyes were narrow slits of contentment. "I feel safe with you, Orla," he said with an extra-big purr.

Orla was just finishing putting on her school uniform on Monday morning. "Now, you'll be fine staying in my bedroom while I'm at—" she stopped as she saw that Flame was already sitting inside her open school bag, an expectant grin on his furry little face.

"Okay. I get the message!" she said, trying not to laugh. He looked so cute and mischievous sitting there with just the tips of his sharp little teeth showing. "Are you sure about this? There'll be lots of kids around. You could get into all kinds of trouble."

"Do not worry about me. Only you will be able to see me," Flame reminded her.

"Well, all right then," Orla agreed. Having Flame with her would make school tons more fun.

The doorbell rang.

"Joe's here," her mom called up the stairs.

"Thanks, Mom. See you later!" Orla cried, going downstairs to meet him. "How was your grandma?" she asked Joe as they set off for school.

"Great. She's lots of fun and a great cook. What happened with Flame? Did your mom and dad let you keep him?" Joe asked eagerly.

"Not exactly. I . . . um . . . told them he belonged to you," Orla admitted.

Joe's eyes widened. "What did you do that for?"

"I had to think of something quickly if I wanted to keep Flame without my parents knowing. I'd already shown him to Grace. And you know what she's like for tattling . . ." She stopped, seeing that Joe looked confused. "Look. All you need to know is that everyone *thinks* Flame lives with you, but he *really* lives with me. I'm hiding him in my bedroom."

Joe's face cleared. "Cool!" he said admiringly.

"If Grace ever mentions a kitten, just remember that you're supposed to be Flame's owner," Orla said. *This is starting to get very complicated*, she thought.

She didn't like telling fibs—and was terrible at it anyway, because she usually forgot what she'd said in the first place. But there was really no choice if she was going to keep Flame safe from his enemies.

In class, Miss Bussell finished taking attendance. "Okay, everyone, nature books out, please. We're going to continue our work on wildlife. I'd like you to start working through exercise four on page thirteen."

As Orla opened her bag, Flame jumped out. He leaped silently and invisibly up onto her desk and then sat there washing his face. Orla smiled. It was still strange to get used to having Flame in full view while knowing that no one else could see him.

Orla glanced up from her workbook to see that Miss Bussell had finished clearing a big bulletin board. She was pinning up a sign, which read "Our Wildlife Photographs."

"After break, we'll start pinning
up your photos. I hope you've all
remembered to bring some," Miss
Bussell said.

"I didn't know we had to!" Orla
whispered to Joe.

"She told us on the bus back to
school after we'd been to Borton Pits,"
he replied.

"Did she?" Orla realized that she must have been too nervous about making sure that no one saw Flame to notice.

Flame came over and jumped into Orla's lap. "Is something wrong?" he mewed worriedly.

She stroked him under her desk. "I was supposed to bring some photos with me for the bulletin board." She bit her lip. "I don't seem to be able to get anything right lately."

"That is not true. You are a very good friend," Flame purred indignantly.

"Thanks, Flame," Orla said, feeling a little better.

As the bell rang for recess, Orla sighed. "Anyway. Let's go over to the playing field. I'd bet you'd love to run around," she whispered to Flame.

As Flame scampered outside after her, Orla didn't notice the thoughtful gleam in his eyes.

Chapter
FIVE

As Orla entered the classroom after recess ended, she heard loud whoops of laughter from a few kids near the bulletin board.

Flame picked up his paws and held his head high, looking very pleased with himself as he ran across the room ahead of Orla.

"What's going on?" Orla wondered,

and then she gasped as she saw the
board.

The whole thing was covered by a
poster-size picture. It was a blown-up,
not-very-good photo of a lot of grass,
with a tiny, startled-looking squirrel in
the bottom corner. Next to it, a neat
card read "Orla Newton. Squirrel in
the Park."

"But? How? When?" Orla
stammered and then the penny
dropped. "Flame!" She looked over to
where he was, beaming proudly at her
from the top of a bookcase.

"Couldn't you have found a bigger
photo?" one of Orla's classmates
commented.

"Or a decent one, anyway!" another
of them said, giggling.

"It was *meant* to be a joke!" Orla
said quickly, going over to take it down.
Rolling it up, she thrust it into her bag
just as the rest of the class and Miss
Bussell came in.

"Quiet, please!" the teacher said,
clapping her hands. "I'd like you all to

get your photos out now and we'll start putting them up."

Orla sidled to the back of the room, wishing like crazy that she was invisible like Flame.

She heard a tiny thud as Flame jumped to the floor and came running over.

"Did I do something wrong?" he mewed worriedly.

Orla glanced down at him. "It's okay, I know you were trying to help. But I think you should leave the photo stuff to me, otherwise it would be cheating," she whispered.

Flame nodded. "I understand."

Orla watched enviously as kids began putting up their photos. There were some really good ones of ducks

and swans and some of birds on feeders
and frogs in ponds.

Joe was one of the last to go over
to the board. He looked over and
winked at Orla as he pinned up his
photo.

Orla frowned. What was Joe up
to? She watched as he pinned up a
photo—of a bare foot!

"Orla? Did you bring—" Miss
Bussell stopped as she caught sight of
Joe's photo. "Joseph Manners! Your
foot's hardly wildlife, is it?" she said
sternly.

"It *is*, Miss!" Joe paused for effect.
"I've got athlete's foot, and Mom says
it's a fungus—just like mushrooms!"

Orla cracked up. The whole class
joined in, and even Miss Bussell looked

as if she was having a hard time keeping
a straight face.

"That is *so* gross!" Orla spluttered.

Miss Bussell clapped her hands for
quiet. "Very funny. But joking around
won't win you any prizes. You can take
that photo down now, Joe!"

"Yes, Miss," Joe said.

"Phew! That was a lucky escape," Orla whispered to Flame as normal lessons started. "Thanks to Joe, Miss Bussell seems to have forgotten all about me, and I won't get told off for forgetting my photos. But I've got to get some good pics soon, or I have no chance of winning that fancy camera. There's only a week left to hand your photos in."

The following Saturday afternoon, Orla sighed as she looked out at the rain-blurred street. "I was hoping we could go out, but I suppose we could always watch some of my *Star Wars* DVDs," she commented.

Flame didn't answer. He was standing

up on his back legs on the windowsill, snapping at a raindrop that was trickling down the glass.

Orla smiled. It was sometimes hard to remember that Flame was a majestic young white lion in disguise.

She reached out to stroke the tiny kitten's little fluffy brown head. "I wish you could live here with me forever."

Flame sat down and turned to face her. "I will stay as long as I can, but one day I must return to my own world and take back my throne. Do you understand that, Orla?" he mewed gently, his green eyes serious.

Orla nodded, but she didn't want to think about that now.

She leaned forward and looked out of

the window. "Hey! It's stopped raining.
We can go out and find some good stuff
to photograph!"

Flame leaped from the windowsill
onto her bed and landed on some of
the wildlife magazines from her aunt
and uncle. With a startled mew, he
skidded straight across the glossy covers,

fell off the bed, and plopped onto the soft bedside rug.

"Oops! Are you okay?" Orla said, trying not to laugh and hurt his feelings.

Flame shook out his ruffled fur. "I am fine," he purred, trying to sound dignified.

As Orla picked up the magazines to put them away, she had an idea. "I know where we can go: Uncle Andy and Auntie Bex's house! They've got a great wildlife garden. I'm going to call them right now!"

Orla's aunt and uncle were delighted to hear from her and invited her over right away.

She went outside to tell her dad.

Mr. Newton looked up from washing

his car. "I'm heading out in a minute to pick up Grace from running club. I can drop you off there if you like," he offered.

"No. It's okay, thanks. I'll walk over," Orla said. She thought Flame would enjoy some fresh air.

She set off with Flame scampering along at her heels. They went in the direction of the park and then turned down a side street. A big road full of stores ran along the bottom. Her aunt and uncle lived on a road that led off that.

Orla slowed down as she and Flame reached the road with all the stores. "I think I'll stop and get a drink and some chips," she said, fishing in her jeans for her allowance.

Four familiar figures came out of the newsstand as Orla approached.

It was the mean girls from the park.

Orla hesitated. But it was too late to turn back. The girls had seen her.

Chapter
SIX

"Well, if it isn't that snotty kid with the camera," the tall blond girl who seemed to be the ringleader sneered.

"Look! She's got a kitten with her this time!" another of the girls said, pointing at Flame.

Orla's heart skipped a beat. They could see Flame! He must have forgotten to stay invisible.

The blond girl came right up to Orla. She stood in front of her with her hands on her hips, blocking the pavement. "Hand over that camera," she ordered.

"I c–can't," Orla stammered nervously. "It's not mine."

"Okay, then. I'll take this instead! I want a new pet!" Before Orla realized what was happening, the blond girl bent down and grabbed Flame with both hands.

Flame mewed with shock and tried to wriggle free, but the girl tightened her hands around his middle.

"Hold still, you little fleabag!" she ordered angrily.

Flame whimpered with pain and lashed his tail.

Orla lunged forward. She grabbed the bigger girl's hands and tried to pry

Flame free. "Give him back! You're
hurting him!"

"Hey! Get off her, you meanie!" One
of the other girls gave Orla a shove.

"Oh!" Orla lost her balance and
stumbled against a wall.

She banged her knee hard, but
she hardly noticed the pain. Her mind
was racing as she tried desperately to

think of a way to get back Flame.
She'd just have to give them her dad's
camera, but then she remembered
her allowance.

She held out a few dollars. "Give
me back Flame, and I'll give you this!"

The blond girl looked undecided,
but then she thrust Flame at Orla.
"Here, have the mangy fleabag."
Grabbing the money, she smirked as
she and her friends walked away.

Orla cradled Flame against her
T-shirt as the girls went into a store
farther down the road. She could
feel him trembling, and his tiny heart
was beating fast against her hand. "It's
okay. You're safe now. Come on, let's
go before those horrible girls come
back out."

"Ow!" Orla gasped at the sudden sharp pain in her knee. Biting back tears, she limped down a side street.

Flame leaned up to put his front paws around her neck. "Thank you, Orla. You were very brave. But you are hurt," he said, blinking in concern. "Quick. Take me into that alleyway."

Orla did as Flame asked. She held on to the wall to steady herself.

As soon as they were alone, she felt a familiar warm prickling sensation down her back as silver sparks ignited in Flame's chocolate-brown fur. He pointed a tiny paw and a fountain of soft pink sparks shot toward her knee. The pain increased for a second, and then Orla felt it draining away, just as if someone had poured it out onto the ground.

"Thanks, Flame! My knee's fine now,"
she said, kissing the top of his fluffy head.

"You are welcome," Flame purred.

"Don't forget to stay invisible from
now on, will you? Especially when
we're with my aunt and uncle," Orla
reminded him.

"Orla! Come on in," Andy Newton said, opening the front door ten minutes later. "Are you all by yourself?"

"Yes, we . . . I mean . . . I walked," she told her uncle as she followed him into the house with Flame in her shoulder bag.

Uncle Andy looked at her closely. "Are you all right, sweetie? You look a little pale."

Orla realized that she still felt a bit wobbly after the encounter with the older girls. "I'm, um . . . just thirsty. Can I have a drink, please?" she said.

"Of course you can. Come into the kitchen. I'll get you one out of the fridge."

Orla wandered in after him. She put down her bag, so Flame could jump out.

"Where's Auntie Bex?" she asked.

"In the garden. Why don't you go on

out and say hello to her?" Uncle Andy
suggested. "I'll bring some cool drinks out
for all of us."

"Okay, thanks." Orla slid open the
big patio doors and Flame followed her
outside. "You're going to *love* exploring
this garden," she said as they passed tubs
of bright orange flowers and clumps of
scented herbs.

Orla started walking across the
enormous lawn, which was dotted with
purple clover. As a butterfly fluttered up
from one of the flowers, Flame gave an
eager mew and darted after it. Orla smiled
and left him to enjoy himself.

"Hi, Auntie Bex!" she called to her
aunt who was standing at the far end
of the lawn near a very complicated
structure.

It had poles of differing heights, some topped with little wooden platforms or tiny houses. Loops of rope were strung between the poles, linking them into a circle. It was a bird-feeding station, Orla realized. She was sure it hadn't been there the last time she'd visited.

"Hello, dear." Bex Newton smiled at her niece. "I'm just filling up these feeders. Do you want to give me a hand?"

"Okay." Orla helped to hang up
some strings of peanuts. "That's an
awesome feeder. You must get zillions of
birds in your garden!" she said.

Auntie Bex grinned. "Maybe not
quite that many, but we do get lots.
Sparrows, blackbirds, wrens, and all sorts
of finches. Your uncle just made this new
feeding station, but it isn't for the birds."

Orla frowned. "What's it for then?"

"For something really unusual that's only been visiting our garden for a week or so and has been stealing the birds' food!" her aunt said mysteriously. "This is an experiment. We thought if we made something especially for our new visitors, they might leave the other feeders alone."

"And is it working?" Orla asked, intrigued.

"I hope you'll be able to see for yourself. They usually visit about this time in the afternoon," said Auntie Bex.

"Really?" Orla's imagination began working overtime. What could the unusual visitors be? "Is it something that's escaped from a zoo?" she asked.

Sitting over by the table, Uncle

Andy laughed. "I don't think so. But you can judge for yourself. Here they come now."

"Look at the plum tree, Orla," her aunt said softly.

Orla saw two slim, dark shapes weaving expertly through the branches. They ran down the trunk, dropped to the grass, and bounded across to the feeding station.

Orla watched delightedly, taking in every detail of the alert bright eyes, tiny paws, and bushy tails. They were squirrels. But she had never seen anything like them.

From the tufted tips of their ears to the ends of their tails they were a glossy coal-black!

Chapter
SEVEN

"Wow! They're *so* amazing!" Orla
breathed, watching the black squirrels on
the feeding station.

They were experts at shimmying
up and down the poles and snaking
across the drooping ropes. One by one,
they leaped onto the tiny platforms and
reached inside the little carved houses,
helping themselves to tasty snacks.

"Aren't they?" Uncle Andy agreed. "We've been watching them performing their acrobatics on that feeder for the last week or so. They've gotten quite used to us sitting here."

"I thought squirrels were always gray or red. Why are these ones black?" Orla wanted to know.

"We don't really know. But we
think it's something to do with genetics.
We once had a blackbird with white
wing feathers in the garden," her
aunt said.

Orla nodded. She had learned about
genetics in science class, and she had
seen albino mice and rabbits with white
fur and pink eyes.

"I'm going to take a photo of the
black squirrels," she said. Very slowly, so
she didn't make any sudden movements,
Orla reached down beside her chair for
her bag. But then she remembered that
she'd left it in the kitchen. "Oh no.
My camera's inside my bag. If I get up
to grab it the squirrels will run away,
won't they?"

"Probably, but don't worry," Auntie

Bex said. "They come here every day
at about the same time. Why don't you
come back tomorrow afternoon?"

"You could come a bit earlier and
get organized," her uncle suggested.
"If you hide yourself over there, you'll
be able to get some really good close-
ups," he said, pointing to a bush with
big pink flowers.

"That's a great idea!" Orla said,
beaming. She couldn't wait to come
back and take some photos of the
unusual black squirrels.

Flame came bounding across
the lawn and curled up under Orla's
chair as her aunt was bringing out
some iced tea. The homemade
cookies and chocolate cake were
delicious.

Orla managed to drop a few cookie
crumbs on the grass for Flame without
anyone noticing.

After their snack, Orla's aunt and uncle
offered to drive her home.

"Thanks very much," Orla said
gratefully. She didn't mind walking, but
she didn't want to bump into those girls
again, especially after how they'd treated
Flame.

As they drove back past the park, Orla
saw a police car parked near the gates. Two
policemen stood on the pavement beside
a familiar group of four girls. A smaller girl
stood there, looking upset, and a woman,
who looked like her mother, was pointing
at the four girls and shouting angrily.

"It looks like someone's in trouble,"
Uncle Andy said, glancing at Orla in the

driver's-side mirror. "Do you know
those girls?"

"Kind of, but not very well," Orla
replied from the backseat. She lowered
her voice and whispered to Flame who
was sitting on her lap. "I bet they've
been up to their mean tricks again, and
the girl's mom's reported them this time.
Serves them right. Maybe they'll stop
picking on smaller kids now!"

"—and I didn't even know there *were* black squirrels! So I bet no one else will have any photographs of them," Orla was telling her dad excitedly as he raked up the yard the following day.

She loved the scent of freshly cut grass. It was a happy summery smell.

Mr. Newton shook his head. "I've never heard of it before, either. I'd love to see them, and I bet your mom would, too. And Grace doesn't have to go to the rec center today, so we could all come with you to see them. What?" he stopped as Orla frowned and folded her arms.

"How am I supposed to get any photos with everyone stomping around the garden like elephants and upsetting

the squirrels? And I *really* I don't need
Grace there giving advice! I'll just get all
nervous and drop the camera again. Like
at Borton Pits—" she stopped guiltily,
but luckily her dad didn't seem to have
noticed.

Mr. Newton began cleaning the
mower. "Hmm. I can see your point. How
about if I drop you off early, and then we
all come along a little later on?"

"Perfect!" Orla exclaimed.

Her mom came to tell them lunch was
ready. Linking arms with her dad, Orla
went into the house.

"Here you are, Flame. I've managed
to get you some lunch." Orla brought a
small dish of steak and potatoes into her
bedroom.

But he wasn't napping on her bed
where she had left him.

"Where are you?" she asked, smiling.
"Oh, I get it! You're playing hide-and-seek.
Coming, ready or not!"

She put the dish down and then
looked for Flame under the bed, in the

closet, and behind the curtains. She
even pulled out the chest of drawers and
looked behind it. But there was still no
sign of him.

"Flame?" she called, beginning to feel
worried.

A very faint whimper came from
the bed. Orla noticed a tiny mound under
the comforter where it lay against the
pillows. She folded the comforter back
and saw Flame's fluffy brown tail sticking
out from beneath her pillow.

"What's wrong? Are you sick?" she
asked, lifting the pillow and stroking him
gently. She could feel Flame trembling all
over and his chocolate-brown fur seemed
dull.

He turned to her with troubled green
eyes. "I can sense my enemies. They are

very close," he whined in terror.

Orla bit back a gasp. She had
been dreading this moment, and now
it was here. Flame was in terrible
danger. Maybe Flame could still stay
with her if she could find a way to
help him.

"I won't let those horrible spies get
you! What about hiding in our garage?
Or I can take you to my aunt and
uncle, and you can hide in their garden
for a few days—"

"No, Orla. It is too late," Flame
interrupted with an urgent little mew.
"If I stay completely still, my enemies
may pass by. Just leave me alone for a
little while, please."

"Well . . . okay, then," Orla said in a
small voice.

Very gently, she tucked the pillow
and comforter around Flame's tiny
form so he was completely hidden
again. She really hated to think of
losing her friend, but she knew she was
going to have to be strong and do as
Flame asked.

"Orla! Are you ready yet? Dad's getting the car!" Grace called impatiently up the stairs.

"Coming!" Orla answered.

As she grabbed her bag and went downstairs, Orla felt her throat tighten with sadness. She hoped like crazy that Flame would still be here when she got back from her aunt and uncle's house.

Chapter
EIGHT

Orla crouched behind the flowering
bush in her aunt and uncle's garden.
She had a clear view of the squirrel-
feeding station.

But although she was trying to feel
excited about seeing the black squirrels
again, her worries about Flame kept
pushing into her mind.

As a faint rustle came from a

nearby flower bed, Orla forced herself
to concentrate. She checked that the
camera was ready. This time, she wasn't
going to mess it up.

A clump of leaves in the flower bed
shook as something ran past them. Orla
held her breath, ready to take a photo at
the first sight of the squirrels.

Here they came!

Orla pressed the button. But instead
of a black squirrel, a cute brown nose
dusted with yellow pollen appeared
followed by two bright emerald eyes
and a pair of pointed chocolate-brown
ears. The tiny kitten sprang out of the
marigolds and landed on the lawn in a
single bound.

"Flame!"

Orla only just managed to stop

herself from laughing out loud with joy and relief as he ran over to her. "You're still here! And I've just taken your photo!"

Flame rubbed himself against her ankles, purring loudly. "My enemies have passed by, but they still might come back. If they do I will have to leave at once."

Behind the bush, Orla picked Flame up and cuddled him. She was so pleased to see him again that she couldn't quite take it in. She just hoped his enemies kept passing by forever.

"I could have sworn the squirrels were in that flower bed," Orla heard her uncle saying.

"They couldn't have been. Here they are now, coming through the

plum tree," her aunt replied softly.

Flame jumped down and Orla
quickly pointed the camera. The
squirrels ran down the plum tree's
trunk onto the lawn and headed for the
feeding station.

Click! Orla took a photo as they
scrambled across a rope. *Click!* She took

another as one of them sat on top of
a pole holding a peanut in its delicate
paws. *Click! Click!* She took more shots
just as one of the squirrels jumped right
into the air, its bushy tail flying straight
out behind it.

"I've really gotten the hang of the
camera now!" she whispered to Flame.

The squirrels leaped and ran and
jumped around on the feeding station
for another five minutes. Finally they
each grabbed a fat peanut and wove
and climbed their way back down onto
the lawn.

Orla kept taking photos, until the
squirrels ran back into the plum tree and
disappeared over the garden fence.

"That was amazing," Orla said to
Flame. "If I haven't got some good

stuff this time, I'll eat Grace's smelly sneakers!" When Flame looked startled, she laughed. "Just kidding!"

Orla felt nervous but excited as her dad drove toward the community center a week later.

"It's great that one of your photos was picked," Mr. Newton said proudly. "I can't wait to see it displayed with the rest of the finalists."

"I know. I can't believe it," Orla said.

"Me neither. It's a complete miracle," Grace murmured.

Orla grinned to herself. Even Grace couldn't dampen her spirits today!

Inside the community center, Orla walked around, holding Flame in her shoulder bag.

Crowds of people moved around,
looking at the display boards. Orla saw
Joe with his parents. He came over
to her.

"Your photo's amazing. It should
definitely win," Joe said.

"Thanks. It's pretty good, right?"
Orla said modestly.

It was the photo of the black
squirrel in midair. Every detail of its
glossy black coat, alert face, and bushy
tail was clearly detailed and in perfect
focus. Mounted on a black board and
with a white border, it looked very
professional.

"Good luck, Orla." Her aunt and
uncle came over to give her a hug.

"Thanks," she said, beaming.

The mayor, wearing a smart purple
suit and a thick gold necklace, was
doing the judging. Orla held her breath
as the mayor walked around, pausing
now and then to examine a photo.

She was coming over! Orla held
her breath. The mayor stopped and put

a yellow sticker on the photo next to
hers.

"What's a yellow sticker mean?"
she asked Joe, as the mayor moved on.

"I think that's third prize. A red
sticker is second, and blue is first," he
replied.

The mayor stopped and looked
at Orla's photo, before moving slowly
past.

"I guess that's it then," Orla said,
trying not to feel too disappointed.
"It's hot in here. I'm going outside for
a minute. I'll see you later."

"I do not think that the judging
is over yet," Flame mewed as Orla
moved down a long corridor toward
the exit. There were lots of rooms on
either side.

"You're not going to do anything magical, are you? Remember what I said about cheating?" Orla said.

"I remem—" Flame's purr ended abruptly.

Orla frowned in surprise and put out her hand to stroke him, but her fingers closed on empty space. She was just in time to glimpse the tiny brown kitten streaking through a nearby door that stood ajar. A notice on the door read STOREROOM.

Suddenly Orla glimpsed fierce, shadowy cat shapes. They were peering into all the rooms.

Flame's enemies had found him!

Orla's heart missed a beat. Without a second thought, she hurried into the storeroom to warn Flame.

A bright white flash blinded her for
a second. Orla blinked hard and then
saw a regal young white lion standing
in front of some stacked chairs.
Thousands of tiny jewel-like sparks
glittered in his glossy coat.

Prince Flame! He was no longer
disguised as a fluffy chocolate-brown
kitten. Orla had forgotten how
magnificent Flame looked as his
true self.

An older-looking gray lion with a
kind, wise face stood beside Flame. "We
must leave now," he rumbled.

"Good-bye, Flame. I'll never forget
you," Orla said, her voice catching in
her throat.

Prince Flame nodded sadly. "You
have been a good friend, Orla."

Orla blinked away tears. Rushing forward she threw her arms around his neck.

Prince Flame allowed her to give him one last cuddle, and then he took a step back. "Be well, Orla. Be strong," he said in a deep, velvety roar.

As Orla waved, there was a final

spurt of bright silvery sparks that hung in the air for a moment before dissolving. Both big cats began to fade, and then they were gone.

Orla heard a growl of rage. She turned to see the dark cat shapes slinking through the doorway and then they, too, disappeared.

Orla stood there, her heart aching. She was relieved that Flame was safe, but she was going to miss him terribly.

Slipping her hand into her pocket, she took out the photo she had taken of Flame jumping out of her aunt and uncle's flower bed. There was nothing there, except a faint, sparkly blurred shape of a young lion. To anyone else it looked like a trick of the light.

But Orla knew it was Flame.

She would always have this reminder of the time she had shared with the tiny magic kitten.

"Orla? Where are you?" called Joe. He grabbed her arm as she came out of the storeroom. "You've won! Come and see. The mayor just put a blue sticker on your photo!"

"Really?" Orla wiped her eyes and hurried after Joe.

As she slipped the precious photo back into her pocket, she felt herself beginning to smile.

About the Author

Sue Bentley's books for children often include animals or fairies. She lives in Northampton, England, and enjoys reading, going to the movies, and sitting watching the frogs and newts in her garden pond. If she hadn't been a writer, she would probably have been a skydiver or brain surgeon. The main reason she writes is that she can drink pots and pots of tea while she's typing. She has met and owned many cats, and each one has brought a special sort of magic to her life.

Don't miss these Magic Kitten books!

Don't miss these Magic Ponies books!